Look for these
ROTTEN SCHOOL
books, too!

#1. The Big Blueberry Barf-Off!

#2. The Great Smelling Bee

#3. The Good, the Bad and the Very Slimy

#4. Lose, Team, Lose!

#5. Shake, Rattle, & Hurl!

#6. The Heinie Prize

#7. Dudes, The School Is Haunted!

#8. The Teacher from Heck

#9. Party Poopers

#10. The Rottenest Angel

ROTTEN SCHOOL

GROWTH · LEARNING · PIZZA!

Punk'd and Skunked

DATE · SCENE · TAKE

R.L. STINE

Illustrations by Trip Park

HarperCollinsPublishers

A Parachute Press Book

Visit us at www.abdopublishing.com

For Chase —TP

Reinforced library bound edition published in 2011 by Spotlight, a division of ABDO Publishing Group, 8000 West 78th Street, Edina, Minnesota 55439. This edition was reprinted by permission of HarperCollins Children's Books, a division of HarperCollins Publishers, 10 East 53rd Street, New York, NY 10022. www.harpercollinschildrens.com

Printed in the United States of America, Melrose Park, Illinois.
092010
012011

 This book contains at least 10% recycled materials.

Library of Congress Cataloging-in-Publication Data
This title was previously cataloged with the following information:

Stine, R.L.
    Punk'd and skunked / R.L. Stine ; illustrations by Trip Park.
        p.   cm. — (Rotten School ; 11)
    Summary: Bernie Bridges and his Rotten School friends win a trip to a local prep school to compete in the National School Make-A-Great-Invention Contest.
    [1. Inventions--Fiction. 2. Contests--Fiction. 3. Boarding schools—Fiction. 4. Schools—Fiction. 5. Humorous stories.] I. Park, Trip, ill. II. Title. III. Series: Stine, R. L. Rotten School ; 11.
PZ7.S86037Pun 2007
[Fic]—dc22   2007006997

ISBN: 978-1-59961-835-7 (reinforced library bound edition)

All Spotlight books have reinforced library binding and are manufactured in the United States of America.

—:CONTENTS:—

Morning Announcements..1

1. PPP.. 3

2. Drooling.. 7

3. How Do You Spell $$$$?.. 10

4. A New Taste Treat.. 13

5. Slap, Slap... 18

6. April~May Makes It Rain.. 24

7. A Solid Platinum Winner.. 29

8. An Inside~Out Nose... 38

9. And the Winner Is ... .43

10. Belzer's PPP Problem.. 45

11. Who's Got the Invention?... 51

12. Don't Make Waves 55

13. A Splash of Tea 61

14. Loser Inventions 69

15. Punk'd and Skunked 75

16. Think . . . Think . . . Think 80

17. Stuck in the Swamp 83

18. An Instant Winner 88

19. A Croquet Lesson 95

20. A Rule Against Naked Butts? 98

21. Sweet! 102

22. A Big Finish 106

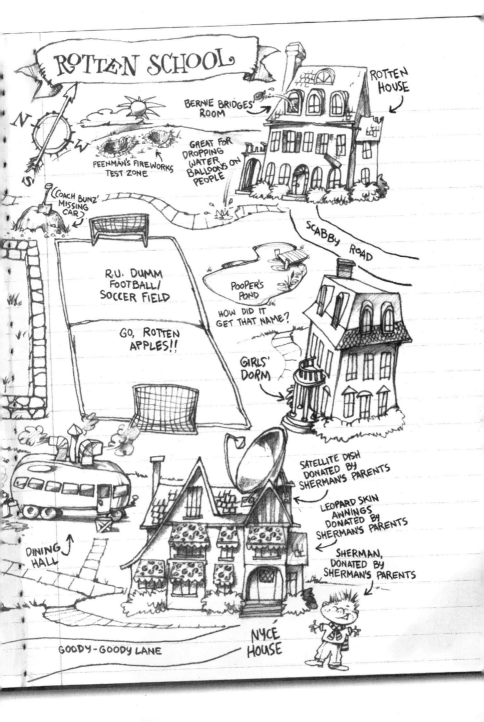

MORNING ANNOUNCEMENTS

Good morning, everyone. This is Headmaster Upchuck, wishing everyone a Rotten Day in every way. Remember—each and every one of you is a Rotten student. And that should make you proud. Here are today's Morning Announcements....

Congratulations to The Bleeders, our varsity Head-Butting team, for winning the State Head-Butting Championship. I'll be handing out the trophy as soon as the boys stop crying and holding their heads.

Chef Baloney announces that tonight is "Not Too Spoiled" Night in the Dining Hall. Chef will be serving tasty leftovers that are not too spoiled. Enjoy!

The Make-a-Great-Invention Contest has begun. I'm sorry that sixth-grade inventor Chris P. Chikken will not be able to show off his clever invention—the Chocolate-Flavored Backpack— because he ate it.

In other Invention Contest news, Nyce House student Wes Updood says he has invented a new day of the week. He calls it Thrukesday. I've asked the nurse to give Wes a thorough checkup.

Our annual Frog Roast will be held Friday night. Anyone interested in roasting a frog should sign up today. The frogs are going fast.

Our school Whistling Champion, Otto Nobetter, will not be performing the "Theme From *Scooby-Doo*" tonight because of a big, red, oozing sore on his lip. Otto will be showing off his sore at lunch today.

2

Chapter 1

PPP

"Dudes, here's a spelling lesson," I told my friends. "How do you spell *excitement?*"

Belzer scratched his head. "Does it start with an X?"

I patted him on the back. "Nice try."

Belzer grinned his lopsided grin. "It was a lucky guess," he said.

"Yo, Belzer," Feenman said. "Do big noses run in your family?"

"I've heard that joke," Belzer said.

Feenman grinned. "Who's *joking?*"

"Give it a rest," I said. I pulled Feenman, Crench,

Belzer, Nosebleed, and Billy the Brain into the Common Room. *"This* is how you spell *excitement,"* I said.

"B~E~R~N~I~E."

That's me, see. I'm Bernie Bridges. Some people call me Grandmaster Dude, King of All the Fourth Graders. But I'd never say anything like that. I'm *waaay* too modest.

But when I have news, I have NEWS. That's why I dragged all my guys into the Common Room. It's a big room with couches and chairs, a TV, and a game table. It's like our living room.

You probably go home every day after school. But Rotten School is a boarding school. That means we *live* here, in a dorm. It's actually a falling down, old house called Rotten House. It's the best dorm on campus—mainly because Bernie B. lives here.

Oops. There I go, being *modest* again!

My friend Beast was chewing a couch cushion. It took three guys to pull him away.

4

Beast is a good guy. But we're not sure if he's really human. He's too hairy to be a human. And last week he got caught chewing his initials into a tree trunk.

I like him. But I keep my fingers away from his mouth.

I stood at the head of the game table. "Dudes, I know you're wondering why I invited you here," I said.

Crench rolled his eyes. "Bernie, we know why," he said. "You want to have a poker game tonight. But we can't."

"We're broke," Feenman said. "You already took all our money. I swear!"

I made a spitting sound. "Forget poker games," I said. "That's small potatoes. I've got something BIG. Something exciting with a capital X!"

Now I had their attention. I pulled open my school blazer so they could see my T-shirt.

They all stared at it. Belzer sounded out the letters.

"Bernie, what's your problem?" Nosebleed asked. "Why does that say *PPP* on it?"

Beast tossed his head back and hee-hawed. "*P-P-P*. Get it? Get it?*"

Crench tugged the front of my shirt. "If you have to go pee-pee, why wear a shirt about it?"

I pushed his hands away. "Crench, what did I tell you about trying to make a joke? Do you want to strain your brain for life?"

"Well, what does PPP stand for?" Billy the Brain asked.

YES! I even stumped the class brainiac!

"I'll tell you," I said.

But it'll take a whole chapter to explain it. Keep reading, everyone....

Chapter 2

DROOLING

I tapped the letters on my shirt. "*PPP* stands for Preppy Prep Prep," I said. "You guys heard of it?"

Belzer scratched his greasy hair. "You mean you don't have to go pee-pee?"

"Preppy Prep Prep," I repeated.

"That snooty prep school across town?" Billy asked.

I flashed him two thumbs-up. "You got it, ace. You heard about this school, right? It's wall-to-wall rich kids. They have servants to carry their fat wallets for them!"

Beast hee-hawed again. "*P-P-P.* Get it?"

"I heard about that school," Crench said. "The kids all have butlers to dress them in the morning."

"They drive to class on Ferrari motor scooters," Feenman said. "Every room has a Jacuzzi. And they have steaks every day for lunch *and* dinner!"

"I heard they have steaks for *breakfast,* too!" I said. "They're filthy rich! Filthy rich! And soon we're gonna be filthy rich, too!"

I couldn't help myself. I started chanting: "Filthy rich! Filthy rich! Filthy rich!"

I guess I lost it a little. I was hopping up and down, my tongue hanging out, drooling on my shirt. Feenman and Crench had to hold me till I started breathing normally again.

"Big B, I don't get it," Nosebleed said. "How are we going to get to Preppy Prep Prep?"

I stared at him. "Haven't you heard about the contest?" I asked.

That's *another* whole chapter. You'd better keep reading, dudes. I'm getting to the good part.

Chapter 3

HOW DO YOU SPELL $$$$?

Beast started chewing the couch cushion again. It was a problem—because three guys were *sitting* on the couch.

"Listen up, dudes," I said. "Haven't you heard about the Make-a-Great-Invention Contest?"

They stared at me.

"All three dorms at Rotten School have to make a great invention," I explained. "The winner goes to Preppy Prep Prep to compete with five other schools."

"Is there a prize or something?" Crench asked.

"You *bet* there's a prize," I said. "The winning inventors get *five thousand dollars* in cash. Did you hear me? Cash. That's spelled $$$$! And you also get to be on TV on MTV-6."

"Wow!"

"Awesome!"

"Totally rad!"

"No way!"

That got 'em excited. MTV-6 is the best MTV channel of all. They don't play music videos, and they don't talk about anything. They just mess around all day, looking cool.

"We're gonna be on TV and win HUGE bucks," I said, rubbing my hands together. "And we'll stay at Preppy Prep Prep and live like spoiled rich kids for a whole week!"

"YEAAAAAA!"

I finally got them totally worked up. They began to chant, "*Bernie! Bernie! Bernie!*" And they picked me up and carried me on their shoulders around the room five or six times.

Finally I got dizzy and had to hop down.

I raised a fist into the air. "On to Preppy Prep Prep!" I shouted.

"We RULE!
Rotten House
RULES!

YEAAAAAA!"

"Bernie?" a tiny voice whispered.

I turned to see Chipmunk, the shyest kid at Rotten School. He was wedged in a corner. He had his hands covering his face. That's just how shy he is. "Bernie, we have a small problem," he muttered into his hands.

"Problem?" I said. "What kind of problem?"

"We don't have an invention."

Chapter 4

A NEW TASTE TREAT

"Do I look worried? No way," I said. "I know we have a genius in this room. One of you guys is gonna come up with the winning invention."

I glanced down the long table. My guys all stared back at me. Some of them chewed their bubble gum tensely. Some of them couldn't chew gum and stare at the same time.

But I knew my pep talk would start them thinking.

"Who's got the big idea?" I asked. "Who's got the invention that's going to take us to Preppy Prep Prep?"

Stare, stare.

Chew, chew.

"Don't all answer at once," I said.

Finally Billy the Brain raised his hand. "I've got one, Bernie."

I knew the dude would come through. He's the school genius. His body weight is eighty-eight percent *brain*. Really. It's been tested.

"What's your invention, Brain?" I said. "Hey—quiet. Listen up, guys."

Billy rubbed his chin. "How about a balloon that runs entirely on air?" he said.

"Keep thinking," I said.

Sometimes I think Billy has the wrong nickname. Sometimes I think he should be called Billy the Stupid Moron.

Belzer jumped to his feet. He was so excited, he swallowed his bubble gum. The bubble gum wad was as big as a sponge. I could see it slide down his throat.

He choked for about five minutes. Then he said, "I've got it, Big B. It just came to me."

"Belzer, tell us," I said.

"A left-handed paper cup." He flashed me his sheepdog grin.

The poor guy really thought he had a great idea. Sad.

"Sit down," I said. "Rest your brain."

I turned to my friend Nosebleed. He had a tissue pressed to his nose. "Nosebleed, what's up?"

"I was thinking too hard," he said. "It gave me a nosebleed." He shook his head. "That always happens."

"URRRRRRRRP!"

Beast let out a roaring burp that made the lights flicker. "Yo! I just invented the BURP!" he yelled. "Hee-hee-hee-hee! Don't anyone steal it. It's MINE!"

"We're not getting anywhere," I said, sighing. "Come on, dudes. We've got to win this thing. Think. *Think!*"

Feenman raised a hand. "I've got an awesome invention, Bernie. You won't believe it."

"I'll believe it, dude," I said. "Tell us!"

"It's a machine that turns you invisible."

"Whoa!" I cried. "Yes! Excellent, Feenman. We'll

definitely win with that. Tell us how it works."

Feenman shrugged. "Beats me. I just think it's a cool idea."

"Maybe you could do it with mirrors," Crench said.

"Keep thinking," I told them.

Billy the Brain jumped up. "This time I've got it, Bernie. Think about this—a reusable toothbrush! Get it? A toothbrush you can use again and again!"

I squinted at him. "Billy, are you from Mars? They're *already* reusable."

His mouth dropped open. "They ARE?"

I looked around the room. "Anybody got an idea? Come on—anybody?"

Beast had a strange grin on his face. His jaw was moving up and down. He started to pant like a dog.

"Beast, you've got an idea?" I asked.

He nodded. "Everyone will love it," he said. "It's so tasty!" His grin grew wider. "It's called Hamster on a Stick!"

"Oooooh—gross!"
"Yuck!"

"Eeeuuuuuw!"
"I'm gonna be sick!"

Guys were gagging and holding their stomachs.

Beast pulled some tiny bones from his mouth. "Hey—try one. The fur gets stuck in your teeth. But it tastes GREAT!"

Chapter 5

SLAP, SLAP

I left Rotten House and took myself for a walk across campus. Maybe the sun was shining, maybe not. Maybe it was a warm day, maybe cold.

I couldn't care less.

I was thinking hard. And when Bernie B.'s brain starts chugging, I can't see or hear anything but my brilliant thoughts.

Once again I had to do all the work. My guys were clueless. I had to dream up something awesome to win the contest.

How about shoes you can also wear as gloves?

A light-up comb so you can see your hair in the dark? Brilliant—but not brilliant enough.

I had my head down as I walked. I was thinking so hard, I could feel my brain turning somersaults in my skull.

"Whoa—" I bumped right into the Peevish twins. Flora and Fauna Peevish are totally identical. They are both short and thin with brown eyes and mousy brown hair.

"Hi, Bernie," Flora said.

How did I know she was Flora? She was the one standing next to Fauna.

"Why don't you watch where you're going?" Fauna asked.

I snapped my fingers. "Awesome!" I said. "That might be an awesome invention. A machine that watches where you're going *for* you!"

Fauna rolled her eyes. "You're entering the Make-a-Great Invention Contest? You've already lost. We're gonna win."

"Are you kidding?" I replied. "I have my suitcase packed. And I'm learning the Preppy Prep Prep school song."

I started to sing the first chorus....

"Where does everyone keep in step, step, step?
At Preppy Prep Prep ... Preppy Prep Prep ...
We've got the P-E-P, and P-E-P spells pep!
No one is shleppy.
We're all just preppy. . . ."

Flora had her hands clamped over her ears. Fauna was chewing her hair.

"Don't worry," I said. "You two won't have to hear that song again. Because you'll be staying here at Rotten School. My dudes and I will be keeping in step, step, step at Preppy Prep Prep."

I started to sing again.

Flora gave me a hard punch in the stomach that stopped the song in mid-*Prep*.

"What's your great invention, Bernie?" Fauna asked.

"Think I'd tell YOU?" I said. "You'd steal it in a second!"

"He doesn't have an idea," Flora told her sister. They both snickered. The Peevish twins have a nasty snicker.

"Well, what's *your* brilliant idea?" I asked.

"Flora and I have an awesome invention," Fauna said. "But we don't know if the other girls will like it."

They both stuck their hands out. They were each holding a long broomstick.

I laughed. "Are you going to fly those to dinner tonight?"

They both rolled their eyes. "Not brooms," Flora said. "Look." They held them higher. At the end of each broomstick was a large, white hand.

"It's a Reacher," Fauna said. "The hand opens and closes."

I squinted at them. "A Reacher?"

"Yeah. For reaching things on a high shelf," she answered. "You stretch out the stick, the hand grabs the thing that's up high, and you can pull it down."

"Not bad," I said.

"And it was all my idea," Flora said.

"No way!" Fauna cried. "I thought of it first!"

"You're dreaming!" Flora cried. "I invented it."

"No—me!"

"Liar!"

"Double liar!"

"OWWW!"

Fauna swung her broomstick and slapped Flora in the face with the big, white hand.

Flora swung her broomstick and slapped Fauna.

SLAP!

"OWWW!"

SLAP!

"OWWW!"

They were slapping each other silly with the big hands.

"Maybe you should call them *Slappers*," I said.

SLAAAP. SLAAP!

I waved good-bye and walked away. And there stood April-May June in front of the girls' dorm. April-May June, the blondest, cutest, blue-eyed-iest girl on campus.

My girlfriend.

If only she didn't *pretend* she didn't like me! If only she wasn't so *shy* when I was around.

"April-May!" I called. "April-May—wait up!"

She turned and started to run.

See? I told you she was shy.

Chapter 6

April-May
Makes It Rain

April-May ran straight into a brick dorm wall. I had her trapped. She crossed her arms in front of her. "What do you want, Bernie?"

I could tell she was happy to see me by the way she curled her upper lip into a sneer.

"You look awesome today," I said.

"You look like the worm I found in my salad," she replied.

See? She couldn't hide how much she liked me.

"What invention is the girls' dorm working on for the contest?" I asked. "Just curious."

24

She stared at me. "It's a germ catcher. We call it Bernie."

I *love* a girl with a sense of humor.

"What's the Rotten House invention?" April-May asked. "Wait. Let me guess. It's a new way to barf through your nose."

Funny? I told you—she's a riot.

"Give up, Bernie. Rotten House can't win," April-May said. "Since you're so curious, I'll tell you what my idea is. It's a rainmaking machine."

I laughed. "For sure," I said. "And at Rotten House we invented a machine that turns dirt into peanut butter!"

She sneered at me again. What a *beautiful* sneer! "You don't believe me? I'll show you," she said.

"You're gonna make it rain?" I said.

"Stand right there. Don't move," she said. She turned and ran into the dorm, her blond ponytail bouncing behind her like a . . . like a . . . like a ponytail.

"She's gotta be kidding," I told myself. A machine that makes it rain? That's totally *insane*.

DRIP. DRIP.

I felt a few raindrops on my shoulder.

DRIP. DRIP. DRIP.

A few more raindrops on top of my head.

"She did it!" I cried. "She can make it rain!"

SPLOOOSH.

"Owwww!" Something hit me hard.

Cold water poured down my hair and my face.

I looked up and saw April-May leaning out a high window. She was dropping water balloons down onto me.

SPLOOOSH!

She had the most *awesome* smile on her face!

My shoes squished as I slumped away. I was drenched. And I still had no idea for an invention.

Shaking off water, I made my way back to Rotten House. I stepped into the front hall and saw Mrs. Heinie, our dorm mother. She was leaning over a table, using a DustBuster. The DustBuster roared as she swept it back and forth.

Mrs. Heinie stopped for a second—tilted back her head—and sneezed.

And it gave me an idea. An AMAZING idea for an invention!

"Thank you, Mrs. Heinie!" I shouted happily. "Thank you! Thank you!"

She wiped the snot off her nose with the back of one hand. "You're welcome," she said.

Chapter 7

A SOLID PLATINUM WINNER

The morning of the contest, Belzer carried my invention to the auditorium. "Careful with that," I said, walking beside him. "It's worth a FORTUNE."

We stepped into the auditorium. "I feel kinda nervous," Belzer said. "URRRRRRP. Oh, no. I just burped up some of my breakfast."

"How many times do I have to tell you? *Peel* your hard-boiled eggs before you eat them!" I said.

I grabbed the invention away from him. I used his T-shirt to wipe the barf off.

The auditorium was packed with Rotten School

kids. I held the invention up high as I walked down the aisle. "Don't cheer now!" I shouted. "Hold your applause till after I win!"

The three judges were already onstage— Headmaster Upchuck, Mrs. Heinie, and Mr. Skruloose, the assistant headmaster. They sat at a long table in front of the curtain.

Headmaster Upchuck is pink and bald and very short. He was sitting on two phone books, but his head still didn't come above the table.

Mrs. Heinie was dressed in the official school colors—puke green, vomit purple, and you-know-

what yellow. She had a sweet smile on her face as she squinted out at the audience through her thick glasses.

Mr. Skruloose is a big, balloon-chested, stiff-as-a-broom, tough-guy dude. He thinks he's in the army or something. He calls every kid *soldier* and makes us march to class—even the first graders.

I saw that spoiled rich kid Sherman Oaks jump onstage. Sherman lives in Nyce House, the dorm we all hate. Sherman is so spoiled and rich, he pays someone to floss his teeth for him. No joke.

I saw what Sherman was doing onstage. He was slipping each judge a hundred-dollar bill. That made me a little tense.

"Don't worry about Sherman," I told

myself. "*No way* this machine can lose!"

I flashed the judges a thumbs-up and gave them my big Bernie B. grin. And I carried my invention backstage.

The guys from Nyce House and the girls from the girls' dorm were standing tensely beside their inventions. They were waiting for the curtain to go up and the contest to begin.

I held my machine up to them. "You can tell a real winner when you see it!" I said. "No one will blame you if you quit now!"

"Where did you find that piece of junk?" Sherman Oaks sneered. "At the trash dump?"

April-May sneered, too. "Bernie, did you make that out of LEGO blocks when you were five?"

Everyone laughed.

The curtain rolled up. We were standing in front of the whole school. "Welcome, Rotten students," Headmaster Upchuck said. "As you know, all three dorms are competing today in the Make-a-Great-Invention Contest. Kids from the winning dorm will go to Preppy Prep Prep for a week."

"My bags are packed, sir," I said. I held up my

machine. "Maybe you'd like to save time and pick the winner now."

The Upchuck ignored me. "Nyce House will go first," he said. "Tell us about your dorm's invention, Sherman."

Sherman stepped forward. He smiled his perfect smile at the judges. He held his invention in one hand. It glowed in the spotlight.

"It's a solid platinum cell phone," he said.

"Very good, soldier," said Mr. Skruloose. "That's a beauty. How did you make it?"

"I didn't make it," Sherman replied. "My parents bought it for me. It's worth five thousand dollars."

Mrs. Heinie squinted at it through her thick glasses. "Oh, my. You mean you didn't invent it?"

Sherman shook his head. "No. But that's not the important part. Let me tell you the important part."

Headmaster Upchuck scratched his bald head. "Important part?"

Sherman nodded. "I'm going to sell the platinum and give *all* the money to you three judges!" he said.

A grin spread over Headmaster Upchuck's pink face. "Oh. Very good," he said. "Very good invention,

Sherman. I like it!"

"Soldier, I *never* take bribes," Skruloose said. "But you've won me over with this one. I salute you!" He gave a snappy, two-fingered salute. "Very clever, soldier. Excellent!"

Mrs. Heinie was smiling, too. "I think we have a winner," she said. "But let's see what the girls invented."

April-May June stepped to one side of the stage with her friend Sharonda Davis. They pulled out a HUGE machine, about eight feet tall. It had pipes and coils and electrical wires, and two long arms with metal pinchers at their ends.

April-May and Sharonda walked offstage and came back pushing a small bed. They lined it up next to the machine.

"Let me show you how this works," Sharonda said. She pushed a button on the machine, and the two pincher-arms started to move.

"Our invention makes the bed for you in the morning," April-May said. "Look. It even fluffs up the pillow."

The two arms straightened the bedcovers. Then

they fluffed the pillow.

"Watch carefully," Sharonda said. "When the machine is finished, it folds up and becomes a couch."

The machine folded in on itself. A huge cushion slid up. The two girls sat down on the couch.

"YEAAAAAAAAA!"

The auditorium roared with applause.

"Pretty good," Headmaster Upchuck said. "Pretty good."

"Not as good as Sherman's phone," Skruloose said. "Of course, the money he's going to give us has *nothing* to do with my decision."

Sherman ran over and pushed another hundred-dollar bill into Skruloose's shirt pocket.

"We should stop here," Mrs. Heinie said. "But I suppose we have to see what my Rotten House boys have done."

Skruloose motioned to me. "Stand at attention, soldier. Show us your invention."

"Oh, wow. It's showtime. Here goes," I said. "Wish me luck, dudes."

Chapter 8

AN
INSIDE-OUT NOSE

I stepped to the front of the stage. "I'd like to start out by singing the Preppy Prep Prep school song," I said. "I learned it because I know that my friends and I will be going there right after we win the contest."

I took a deep breath and started to sing.

"Where does everyone keep in step, step, step?
At Preppy Prep Prep . . . Preppy Prep Prep . . ."

Some kids started to hiss and boo. Guys screamed for me to stop. Fights broke out.

"SOLDIER, JUST SHOW US THE INVEN-
TION!" Skruloose bellowed, waving a fist in the air.

"The invention?" I said. "But I have six more
verses of the song."

"BOOOOOO!"

"Okay, okay. Here it is," I said, holding it high. "I
know it's brilliant. You don't have to cheer or
applaud."

"What is it?" Mrs. Heinie asked.

"It's a battery-powered Nose Vac," I said. "You
know. Sometimes it's hard to blow your nose. Or
your nose is feeling kinda stuffed up. But you're in
class, so you can't really pick it."

All three judges squinted at me in silence. I guess
they were totally impressed.

"This has 1000-horsepower suck-ability," I said.
"You hold this nozzle up to your nose, flick it on—
and it suctions out your nose so you'll never have to
blow it again."

Headmaster Upchuck shook his head and
frowned. "I think we've seen enough," he said.

"Get off the stage," Mr. Skruloose growled.

"No, wait," I said. "I have a demonstration. I

think this will impress you a lot."

I called my buddy Feenman out onstage. "Feenman, how's your nose?" I asked.

"All stuffed up," Feenman said, just as we had rehearsed. He sniffed, then gave out six or seven really loud sneezes. By the time he finished, I was soaking wet.

"Don't overdo it," I whispered. I turned to the audience. "Watch how the Nose Vac quickly takes care of the problem."

I clicked it on. The machine let out a roar. I raised it to Feenman's nose. The Nose Vac roared and kicked.

Feenman's eyes bulged—and he opened his mouth in a HOWL of pain!

"YOOWWWWWWWWWWW!"

I struggled to pull the Nose Vac off—but it was *stuck to his nose!*

"Get it off! Get it OFF!" he shrieked.

I tugged it and twisted it and pulled with all my strength.

"OWWWWW! It hurts! It HURTS!" Feenman wailed.

"Shhhh. Quiet," I said. "You're ruining our chances."

"MY NOSE! MY NOOOOOOOSE!"

Finally, I clicked the Nose Vac off and dropped it to the stage. Feenman raised a hand to his nose. "It's *inside out!*" he shrieked. "You turned my nose INSIDE OUT!"

I kept a big grin on my face. "It's supposed to do that!" I told the judges. "That's Step One."

"YOWWWWWWWWWWW!"

Feenman held his nose and wailed in pain.

"That scream—that was Step Two!" I said.

"Hurry—get Feenman to the nurse!" Mrs. Heinie cried.

"Okay, okay. The Nose Vac has a few bugs," I said. "But it's still the *best*—right?"

Headmaster Upchuck climbed to his feet. "The judges have reached a decision," he said.

Chapter 9

AND THE WINNER IS...

A hush fell over the auditorium. Everyone was silent—except for Feenman, who was still screaming and holding his inside-out nose.

"The girls' invention is the best!" Upchuck announced.

April-May and Sharonda and all the girls in the auditorium went wild, cheering and shouting, jumping in the air and slapping high fives.

"We're going to PPP!" they cheered. "We're going to PPP!"

I fell to the floor on my knees. I buried my face in

my hands. I could feel my heart breaking in two.

"We're going to Preppy Prep Prep!" Sharonda shouted.

"No, you're not," Headmaster Upchuck said.

The room grew silent again.

"The girls' invention is the best," Upchuck said. "But who *cares*? Do you really think I'd give up a chance to *get rid* of Bernie Bridges for a *whole week?*"

I raised my head. I climbed back to my feet. What was he saying?

"I've been dreaming of this moment!" Upchuck said. "I've tried locks on my door. I've tried locks on *Bernie's* door! I've tried electric fences! I've tried voodoo dolls! *Anything* to keep Bernie away. And today . . . today my dream has come true. A whole week without Bernie Bridges!"

My mouth dropped open. I cupped one ear. Was I really hearing what I was hearing?

"Bernie's invention *stinks!*" Upchuck said. "But I don't *care!* Bernie and his friends are going to Preppy Prep Prep. Good-bye, boys, and good luck!"

Chapter 10

BELZER'S PPP PROBLEM

A week later, Feenman, Crench, Belzer, and I stared out the windows as our bus pulled up to the Preppy Prep Prep campus. We gazed at a field of white and yellow flowers, a wide, green lawn, tennis courts, and tall buildings covered in ivy.

Two girls trotted past us on horseback. "Check out the stables over there," I said, pointing to a long, red-roofed building.

"Bernie, what are those kids doing with those hammers?" Belzer asked.

I squinted out at the lawn. "Those aren't hammers.

They're mallets. They're playing croquet," I said.

"Can you hit each other with those things?" Belzer asked. "That would be *cool!*"

The bus came to a stop. The four of us eagerly jumped off.

A boy and a girl came running across the parking lot to greet us. They both had wavy blond hair and blue eyes and big smiles on their tanned faces. They wore their official PPP school uniforms—white polo shirts and khaki shorts.

"We're the Welcoming Committee," the girl said. "I'm Alli Katz, and this is my friend Corky Pigge."

I flashed them *my* best smile, the one with the adorable dimples. Then I introduced myself and my three buddies.

"What happened to your nose?" Alli asked Feenman. "It's totally inside out."

"A tiny accident," I said. "No big deal. He can still breathe through his mouth."

Alli pulled out a clipboard. She thumbed through several pages. "Your bus is two minutes late," she said. "But we can make up the time." She kept tossing her blond hair back over her shoulders as she scanned the pages on her clipboard.

"I have your schedules here," she said. "I marked off your free times and your work times."

"Alli is very organized," Corky said.

"I signed you up for several activities," she said. "We have an after-school work program I know you'll want to be part of."

"Huh? *Work?*" Crench cried. "Is she kidding?"

I clamped a hand over his mouth.

"I have you staying in Pigge House," Alli said. "I think you'll like it there."

"Pig House?" I said.

Corky nodded. He had a stubby nose, which he kept stuck up in the air. "It's named after my great-great-grand-pater," he said. "My family is one of the founding families of PPP. There's been a Pigge at Preppy Prep Prep for over two hundred years!"

"Awesome," I said.

Feenman giggled. I clamped my *other* hand over *his* mouth.

"I know all the school traditions," Corky said. "Tuesday is Wear Clean Underwear Day. Don't forget that. We gargle with mineral water on every other Thursday. And do you know the shoelace rule?"

"Don't think I do," I said.

"Shoelaces are worn *inside* the shoe," Corky said. "Never outside." He showed me his shoes. I couldn't see any shoelace.

Alli thumbed through more pages on her clipboard. "I've drawn you maps of the campus," she said. "And floor maps of each building. I outlined the paths to the classroom buildings in yellow."

"I told you, Alli is very organized," Corky said again.

Alli handed out our schedule sheets. "I made a list of several good times for you to go to the bathroom."

"How about *now?*" Belzer asked. "That was a *long* bus ride!"

Alli checked her clipboard. "Sorry. Not on the schedule."

Chapter 11

WHO'S GOT THE INVENTION?

"First is the campus tour," Alli said. "We will walk exactly three quarters of a mile. That will be one thousand, two hundred, and forty-two steps. Follow me."

We started to walk across the lawn. "That's where you'll park your motor scooters," Alli said. She pointed to a long row of scooters. "I've assigned four bikes, and I wrote down the serial numbers for you."

"Beats walking!" I said.

"That lake over there is Pigge Lake," Corky said. "It's named after my great-great-great-grand-mater.

Pigges have always loved the water."

"It's a sailboat lake," Alli said. "You know. For radio-controlled sailboats."

"Cool. Can you sink 'em?" Feenman asked.

"He's joking!" I told Alli. "Feenman loves to joke."

"I love to sink things!" Feenman said.

Alli pointed to an ivy-covered building with a wide, outdoor patio. "That's Crumpet Hall," she said. "That's where we have afternoon tea."

I flashed her another winning Bernie B. grin. "I think we'll feel right at home here," I said.

"I set up laptops in your rooms," Alli said. "And I downloaded your schedules."

Crench's mouth dropped open. "We each get our *own room?*"

"Of course," Corky said. "You don't *share* a room at your school, *do* you? Yuccch. That's so unsanitary!"

I pointed to six kids in shorts and white PPP T-shirts running around an asphalt track. "Who are *they?*" I asked.

"We all warm up on the track for an hour every day," Alli said. She checked her clipboard. "Let's see ... I have you down for jogging at 6:30 to 7:30 every morning."

"Perfect!" I said. "Of course, Belzer will be jogging for me. My knees ... my knees ... a bad mountain-climbing accident." I staggered a bit so she'd get the idea.

Corky turned to me. "Didn't you bring your invention? Where is it?"

"You mean our *winning* invention!" I said. "Belzer has it. Belzer, show it to them."

Belzer stared down at his empty hands. His face turned green, then pale white. He swallowed ten or twelve times. "Bernie, I ... I don't have it. I thought *you* had it."

"Feenman? Crench? Did you bring our brilliant invention?" I asked.

They both shrugged. Feenman giggled. "Oops."

"Do you believe it? We forgot our invention," I told Alli and Corky.

Alli frowned. "Oh, wow. You need to think up a new one right away."

Sure, we messed up. But Bernie B. doesn't know the word *defeat*. I grinned at Alli and Corky. "We have a *million* awesome ideas," I said. "All winners! Total winners! I can't wait to start!"

"Well . . . first you have to see the headmaster," Alli said.

"Huh?" Feenman cried. "The headmaster? But we haven't *done* anything really bad yet!"

Chapter 12

DON'T MAKE WAVES

Headmaster Snute was a kindly looking old dude. He was dressed in the school uniform—white polo shirt and khaki shorts. And he had a beat-up, straw fishing hat on his head.

He didn't see us enter his office because he was leaning over a fish tank on his desk.

He held a small fishing pole in one hand. The line dangled into the fish tank. Suddenly he snapped it back with a cry: "Gotcha, you sea devil!"

He stared at the empty hook—then saw us. He smiled. "Ever go fishing for wild guppy?" he asked.

"You have to outsmart them. The wild guppy is one of your faster fish."

I flashed him my best smile. "My dad is a sportsman like you, sir," I said. "He loves to fish, too. But he usually goes *outside* to fish."

Snute squinted at me. "Outside? You can fish *outside?* Are you sure?"

He gazed down at his crowded little fish tank. "I keep it well stocked with goldfish," he said. He licked his lips. "Mighty tasty!"

"These are the contest winners from Rotten School," Alli said. "You wanted to see them?"

"We didn't *do* anything!" Feenman cried. "Really. You can't blame us! We just got here!"

The headmaster chuckled. "I wanted to welcome you all to Preppy Prep Prep. Jump in. The water is fine!"

He reached into a desk drawer and pulled out a stack of disks. "These DVDs are for you," he said. "They have information about our school. You don't want to dive into the water till you know how to swim—right?"

"There's a DVD player in every room," Corky

Pigge said. "And a flat-screen, plasma TV. My family paid for them all."

"Cool!" Crench said. "Are we supposed to take them home when we leave?"

Snute frowned at him.

"He's joking, sir!" I said. "We joke a lot at Rotten School. It's one of our traditions."

"Interesting," Snute said. "We've never tried jokes here. Hmmm ... think they might make a splash?"

"Would you like to hear a joke, sir?" I asked. "A grizzly bear and a chicken go into a restaurant, and—"

"I don't think so," he said. "You boys will find it different here. This is a much bigger pond than you're used to. Be careful not to swim against the current. And watch out for bottom-feeders."

"Bernie," Feenman whispered. "What is he *talking* about?"

I shrugged. "Beats me."

"Don't clam up, boys," Snute said. "The world is your oyster—if you don't make waves."

"Totally right, sir," I said. "We're looking forward to the Make-a-Great-Invention Contest."

He dropped his fishing line into the tank. "The guppies just aren't biting today," he muttered. "But I'm not complaining. PPP is such a wealthy school, I have three assistants who do all my work. Leaves me plenty of time for fishing."

"I'm sorry to interrupt," Alli said, shuffling through the pages on her clipboard. "But these guys are one minute and forty-five seconds behind schedule. We have to hurry up and—"

Before she could finish, a chubby, red-haired boy came running into the office. He shoved a fat envelope at the Headmaster. "Here's the money I collected, Mr. Snute," he said.

Snute took the envelope and set it down on his desk. "Good work, Feldspar."

"Hi. I'm Feldspar Pyrite," the boy said. "Are you in fourth grade? I skipped fourth grade. Everyone in my family always skips fourth grade. We're wacky that way."

He turned back to the headmaster. "This is the money I collected for the Bow Tie Fund. To buy bow ties for the poor. Don't thank me, sir. You know how deeply I care about getting bow ties for the poor. I start to cry every time I think about it." He brushed away a tear.

Was this guy for REAL?

I couldn't resist. I picked up the money envelope. It weighed a *ton!*

Alli checked her stopwatch. "We're late for afternoon tea," she said. "Let's go, guys."

Headmaster Snute waved good-bye. "Don't just flop around. Throw a wide net, boys," he said, "and see what you catch."

We started for the door.

"Aren't you forgetting something?" the headmaster called.

"Oh, yes. Sorry," I said. I pulled the money envelope out from under my shirt and handed it back to him.

Chapter 13

A SPLASH OF TEA

"But I don't *like* tea," Belzer complained. "Yuck. It tastes like ... tea."

"Just pretend to drink it," I said. "We want to make friends—right? You can spit it on the floor when no one is looking."

Back at Rotten School, guys always spit their dinner onto the floor when no one's looking. The food is totally gross. Even the *flies* don't go near it.

We followed Alli and Corky to the terrace of Crumpet Hall. We sat down at a table with a white tablecloth and little china plates. Feldspar Pyrite pulled out a chair and sat down with us.

"Afternoon tea is an old school tradition started by the Pigges," Corky said. "Pigges have been cupping for centuries."

Cupping?

"We only have ten minutes and forty-two seconds," Alli said, checking her clipboard. "Then I have to check you into your rooms."

Feldspar tossed back his head and sneezed. "Bad allergies," he said. He wiped his nose with a five-dollar bill.

My tongue rolled out, and I started to pant.

A tall waiter in a white uniform brought a pot of tea and a tray of little sandwiches.

Feenman grabbed a bunch of sandwiches before the waiter set the tray down. "Hey—these sandwiches don't have crusts!" he cried.

"We don't like crusts on our sandwiches," Corky said, his stubby nose raised in the air. "Too crusty."

He grabbed the teapot. "I'll pour," he said. "Pigges always pour the tea."

Alli stared at her watch. "Eat fast," she said. "I have a list of fourteen more things to do this hour.

After that, I get *really* busy!"

Feenman pawed through all the sandwiches. "Isn't there any salami?"

Belzer took a sip of tea, gurgled it around in his mouth, then tried to spit it on the ground. But he missed and spit it all over Crench.

Crench let out a cry. He grabbed a cheese sandwich and smushed it into Belzer's face. Feenman squeezed a fat glob of tuna salad into Crench's shirt pocket.

Feldspar leaned across the table to me. "Like to play croquet?" he asked.

My buddies started to hoot and laugh. But I shut them up fast.

"Croquet is our favorite sport," I said. "We're on the croquet team at Rotten School. We can't get enough of it...the smell of the fresh-cut grass...the *thwack* of a mallet...thrilling!"

"Maybe we could play a few rounds," Feldspar said.

"We'd love to," I said.

"Maybe a dollar a wicket?" Feldspar whispered. "You know. A little bet to make it more fun?"

I gasped. "Huh? Gamble?" I said. "Oh, no. We're not here to bet on games. We have to concentrate on winning the contest."

"How about we make it *five* dollars a wicket?" Feldspar said.

Oh, wow. I didn't want to bet on croquet. I had my eye on the five-thousand-dollar contest prize. But...I couldn't pass up a bet.

"Well...maybe," I said.

Feldspar reached into his shorts pocket and pulled out a deck of cards. "Here's another game you might like," he said. "It's called poker. Ever play?"

I shook my head. "Poker? No. I've only seen it on TV."

It was a white lie. I really didn't want to get into a card game. It was gonna take all my brainpower to think up a new invention.

"I'll teach it to you," Feldspar said, shuffling the deck like a pro. "Alli and Corky can play, too. Just a fun game."

"I think I can fit it in between eight and eight-twelve," Alli said.

"Maybe we'll play for a few nickels," Feldspar

said. "Or maybe dollars. Just for fun. Meet me in the game room tonight."

This guy Feldspar Pyrite reminded me of someone I liked—ME!

He hurried away. Alli and Corky went to talk to some friends.

I turned to my buddies. They were pouring tea onto each other's heads. "Cool it," I whispered. "Did you hear what I told him? I told him we never played cards before."

SPLASH.

SPLASH.

"OWWWWWW!"

"OWWWWWWW!"

"Know why I told him that?" I said. "Because we don't have time for cards. We've got five thousand dollars to win. Start thinking about an invention, guys. Have you ever heard of an *emergency*? This is it!"

They didn't hear a word I said. They were too busy pouring hot tea on each other and screaming their heads off.

Chapter 14

LOSER INVENTIONS

Motor scooters whizzed past us as Alli led the way to Pigge House, our dorm. Kids flew kites. Kids sunbathed on blankets on the lawn. A group of serious-looking dudes crept by silently, holding binoculars up to their eyes.

"Are they *spies?*" Feenman asked Alli.

She laughed. "No. They're bird-watchers. There's a rumor that a blue-bottomed, fat-breasted wren is on campus."

She smiled at Feenman. "Are you into birds?"

Feenman thought about it. "Well...I eat fried

chicken," he said. "Does that count?"

We stopped in front of a bunch of kids who were working hard, building something very tall. It looked kinda like a *house*.

"What's up with that?" I asked a tall, skinny guy, who was working hard in a T-shirt and shorts. "You building a new dorm?"

He stopped hammering. "Yo. We're the contest winners from

Baked Potato Chips Middle School. This is our project for the Make-a-Great-Invention Contest," he said. He mopped his forehead with one hand.

"What is it?" I asked.

"It's pretty simple," he said. "Inside is a new kind of elevator. This is a small one, but one day we hope skyscrapers will have them. It's powered by human breath."

"Wow!"

"Amazing!"

"Unbelievable!"

My three buddies went nuts.

"Yeah, I thought of doing that," I said. "But it's a little too simple for us. We need more of a challenge."

We walked on. Crench hurried to catch up to me. "Big B, we're in major trouble," he said. "They're building an awesome elevator. And we don't have one idea."

"Don't worry about it," I said. "We'll think of something."

I could picture that five-thousand-dollar prize. And my buddies and me hanging out at MTV-6.

We *had* to think of something fabulous!

At the edge of the lawn, we came to another group of hardworking kids. They were working on a contraption with a big metal loop at the top. Three guys were making a fan for it. Other kids worked on an electronic control.

An awesome-looking girl smiled at me. She had dark eyes and long, dark hair and was wearing tennis shorts and a white polo shirt.

"That's my friend Nicki," Alli said. "Nicki Toros. She goes to Poly-Wannacracker Academy."

"I've *heard* of that school," I said.

"Can you guess what our invention is?" Nicki asked.

"Does it receive radio messages from Mars?" I asked.

"It's the world's best bubble-blowing machine," she said.

"Awesome!" Feenman said. "I blew bubbles for my social studies project."

She stared at him. "You're joking, right? What grade did you get?"

"An F," Feenman said. "But it was my best project all year."

"How does the bubble machine work?" Crench asked, scratching his hair.

"You pour the liquid in here," Nicki said. She pointed to a jar on the back. "Then the fan blows the bubbles into the air. They're as big as beach balls. They're made of plastic. They last for *weeks*."

"Not bad," I told her. "You'll probably come in second—after us."

Her dark eyes flashed. "Why? What's your project?"

I raised a finger to my lips. "*Ssshhh!* Lots of kids here would like to *steal* our idea. I wish I could give you a clue. But our project is too exciting to talk about. We don't even talk about it to *each other!*"

"What school do you go to?" she asked.

"Rotten School," I said.

"Figures," she said.

Chapter 15

PUNK'D AND SKUNKED

Did we win big-time at the poker game? Does a bear barf up its dinner in the woods? Does a guppy take his vacation in a fishbowl?

Of COURSE we won big-time.

I know. I know. I said we weren't going to play. But Bernie B. just couldn't say no.

Feldspar, Corky, and Nicki showed up to play. Belzer had a stomachache from swallowing a chicken leg whole at dinner. So it was just Feenman, Crench, and me. We found a table in a quiet corner of the game room.

Check it out. This was not like the game room at Rotten School—two card tables, a candy vending machine, and a Ping-Pong table.

The game room at this school looked like a huge electronics store. Every video and arcade game you could think of—and big flat-screen monitors to play them on. I saw pinball machines and a bowling alley, Skee-Ball, and a basketball court.

That's a game room! How did these rich dudes ever get to class?

Feldspar shuffled the cards. "So, you guys have never played poker before?" he asked.

"Is it anything like Go Fish?" I asked.

"A little," he said.

"Gambling! I feel so *bold*!" Corky said. "Maybe I'm starting a new Pigge family tradition tonight!"

Feldspar piled a big stack of poker chips onto the card table.

"I've never played with those little plastic things," I said. "Is it hard?"

"Let's keep it simple," Feldspar said. "We'll just use the dollar chips." He started to deal the cards.

"Is it good to have a five?" Corky asked.

"What does a two count for?" Nicki asked.

My heart was pounding. I didn't want to do it. I knew I should be back at the dorm, dreaming up an invention. But my fingers were itching! I had to play. And I had to win. It's in my blood.

I'll skip the gruesome details. Two hours later I had a big grin on my face and two tall stacks of chips in front of me.

The three Preppy Prep Prepsters didn't look happy. They were moaning and making soft, whimpering sounds. I saw teardrops on their polo shirts.

"I'm sorry," I said. "Wouldn't you know it? I had all the luck tonight." I counted the chips. "You owe me twenty dollars each," I said. "Pay up."

The three of them pulled out their wallets.

"Do you have change for a hundred?" Feldspar asked.

"Huh?" I stared at the hundred dollar bill in his hand. "No. I...uh..."

"The smallest I have is a five hundred," Corky said. "Can you change it?"

"I just have credit cards," Nicki said. "I never carry cash."

Whoa. She's in fourth grade, and she only carries credit cards?!

"I don't have change," I said. I forced a smile to my face. "Besides, I'd never take your money. We were just playing for fun—right?"

"We can donate the money to charity," Feldspar said. "How about the Bow Tie Fund?"

I sighed. "Yes," I said weakly. "Bow Ties for the poor. Such a good cause."

They put their money and their credit cards back in their wallets and hurried away.

Feenman, Crench, and I couldn't move. We stayed hunched at the table, staring sadly at the piles of chips.

"We got nothing," Crench muttered. "Zero. *Nada*."

"We've been punk'd and skunked," Feenman said.

I looked up and saw Alli and Feldspar running back to us. "By the way, guys," Alli said. "I hope you downloaded the schedule. Round One of the Make-a-Great-Invention contest is first thing tomorrow morning."

I started to gasp, but I held it in and made it look

like a burp. "Round One?" I asked.

She nodded. "Yes. The judges will look at all five inventions. The kids whose invention comes in last will be *out*. They'll have to go home."

"But we just got here!" Feenman cried.

Feldspar grinned at us. "Hope I didn't keep you guys up too late," he said. And he winked.

Feldspar did it deliberately, I realized. He kept us here playing cards to keep us from working on our invention.

Clever. The guy was as clever as someone else I knew—ME.

We really *had* been punk'd and skunked!

Chapter 16

THINK...
THINK...THINK...

Time for Bernie B. to give a pep talk. I paced back and forth in my dorm room. "Okay, guys," I said. "I know it's already two in the morning. But we're gonna stay up all night and build a fabulous invention. Right?"

No answer.

Feenman and Crench were leaning against each other, asleep on the couch. Belzer lay flat on his back on the floor, snoring away.

"Bad attitude, guys," I said. I shook them awake. "After tomorrow, only four schools will be left in the contest. And we want to be one of them. So start thinking."

Belzer sat up and yawned. "How about an invention that helps you sleep?" he moaned. He dropped back onto the floor.

I shook all three of them some more. I tickled them. I slapped their cheeks. I put ice cubes down their backs.

I work hard for my guys.

Finally I pulled them to their feet. "It's for your own good," I said. "You want to be looking cool on MTV-6, don't you?"

They nodded.

"Start thinking," I said. "If we get a good idea, we can catch a few hours of sleep."

"I've got an awesome idea," Feenman said. He grabbed the flat-screen TV on the dresser. "We take this to the contest and say we invented it."

"Feenman, go back to sleep," I said.

He blinked several times. "How about a shirt you can wear on your head?"

"How about you go back to sleep?" I said.

"Bernie, how about shoes with an alarm in them?

You know. Like a car alarm. In case someone tries to steal your shoes?"

"Feenman, does your head feel hot?" I said. "I think you've overheated your brain."

He felt his forehead. "You think so?"

Crench snapped his fingers. "I got one, Big B! It's a toothbrush, see. But it has a brush on *both* ends. That way, you can brush both sides of your mouth at once."

I patted Crench's shoulder. "You can go back to sleep, too."

Belzer was already asleep.

I knew it. I knew it would come down to my brilliant brain.

Time for me to come up with something awesome and save the day for me and my good buddies.

Think, Bernie … think … *think*. …

YAWWWWWWWWN.

When I woke up, it was 8:20 the next morning.

We had ten minutes. Ten minutes to get cleaned up, changed, make an invention, and get to the science lab for Round One.

Chapter 17

STUCK IN THE SWAMP

"Settle down, people. People! People! Settle down."

Mr. Spittup, the contest judge, was trying to get everyone quiet. He was a young guy, with perfect wavy brown hair, thick eyebrows over green eyes, a flashy smile, an excellent tan, and a silver ring in one earlobe. He wore a white shirt open at the neck over straight-legged jeans.

The kids in the contest gathered in groups around the tables in the science lab. A mobile of the solar system planets hung low over our heads.

Belzer wasn't watching where he was going and

smacked his head on Neptune.

"Settle down, people. Are all five schools here?" Mr. Spittup said. "I can't *wait* to see what you've come up with."

"Neither can I," I muttered.

How did this happen? I glanced around the room. The other four schools all had interesting inventions with them. And my buddies and I stood there with ... with ... nothing.

I needed an idea. I could hear my brain plopping weakly inside my skull. *PLOP ... PLOP ... PLOP ...* The inside of my head felt like a swamp this morning. No ideas could rise out of the muck.

"Good luck to everyone. Let's start with our friends from Poly-Wannacracker," Mr. Spittup said. "Show us your invention."

Nicki Toros smiled and patted her machine. "This will change the sport of bubble blowing forever," she said. "And ... no more children crying when their bubbles pop. Because these bubbles *can't* pop."

Mr. Spittup nodded. "Tough bubbles," he muttered. "Tough bubbles. I like it!"

Next, the kids from Baked Potato Chips Middle

School showed off their air-driven elevator. "You just blow into this pipe, and the elevator car goes up one hundred floors."

"Well done," Mr. Spittup said. "Very clever. Very clever." He breathed into the pipe, and we all watched the elevator rise.

"Next let's hear from our friends here at Preppy Prep Prep. What did you bring us?"

A tall, skinny blond boy stepped forward, bobbing his head. "Yo, yo," he said. "Yo. We'll take first prize now if you'd like to save some time, yo."

Everyone laughed.

Mr. Spittup squinted at their invention. "It looks like a paper airplane," he said.

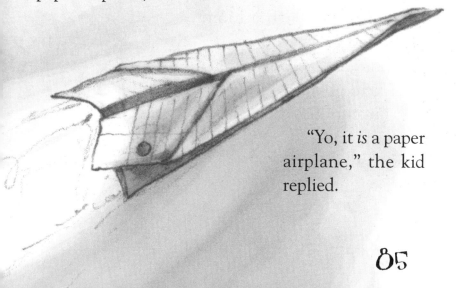

"Yo, it *is* a paper airplane," the kid replied.

"It's radio-controlled, yo. It can fly across the ocean if the wind is right," he said. "Yo."

"I'm impressed," Spittup said. "And what is the paper airplane made of?"

"Paper," the kid answered. "Yo."

Spittup rubbed his chin. "Interesting…"

Was I next? My throat felt tight. My hands started to shake. My brain was gurgling and plopping. I had nothing. NOTHING.

"Our fourth school is the Whussup School," Spittup announced. "Whussup with you guys? Ha-ha."

I let out a sigh of relief. I still had a few seconds to dream up something.

Spittup moved to the Whussup table. "What did you invent?" he asked.

A cute girl with a long, brown ponytail and brown glasses held up some kind of brush. "Our invention is a new kind of toothbrush," she said.

"See? It has a brush at both ends. This way, you can brush both sides of your mouth at once."

"Ouch!" I shouted because Crench elbowed me in the ribs.

"They stole my idea!" he whispered. "I *knew* it was an awesome idea!"

No time to answer Crench. Spittup was smiling at us now and walking over to our table. "And now, last but not least, let's see what our Rotten School friends have brought us," he said.

I gulped. I gulped again. I choked for a minute or two. Stalling. Stalling...

"Well..." I said.

I could hear my swampy brain going *PLOP... PLOP...PLOP.*

Chapter 18

AN INSTANT WINNER

"I know you Rotten School guys have come up with something clever," Mr. Spittup said. "Please share it with us."

I cleared my throat. "Well…uh…"

I gritted my teeth, trying to get the great Bernie B. brain unswamped. *Come on, Bernie, you can fake it. You can always fake it!*

I took a deep breath. "We've been inspired by your school, sir," I started. "Uh . . . Being here has helped us to clear our minds and think deeply about our invention."

Sweat poured down my face. My knees knocked together. How long could I stall?

"Just show us your invention," Spittup said.

"Yes, our invention," I said. "You've been so kind to us. We want to show you our very best work. Uh… We put many hours of thought and labor into our invention…"

I glanced over at Feenman. He was stressed, too. He had a clump of dust the size of a softball in one hand. He was pulling at it, stretching it out.

Yes! YES!!!

"This is our invention," I said. I grabbed the dust ball from Feenman and held it high so everyone could see it. "You know how little kids like to make dust bunnies? Well, we call our invention *Instant Dust*. See? You can model it into any kind of animal you want."

I twisted the dust ball into a little bunny.

Some kids oohed and aahed. My three buddies grinned proudly, as if they'd been working on the invention for weeks.

"Clever. Very clever," Mr. Spittup said. He took

the dust from me and twisted it around for a few minutes. "Look! I made a cat!"

He handed it back to me. "Very clever," he said again. "Instant Dust. I don't know how you ever came up with that."

"Just pure brainpower, sir," I said. I mopped the sweat off my face with a shirtsleeve.

Mr. Spittup paced back and forth in front of us. "I knew I'd have a tough time judging today," he said. "I'm sorry that only four schools can go on to the finals tomorrow. And we will sadly have to say good-bye to one school today."

He walked around from table to table. "Let me check out your inventions one more time," he said.

He worked the bubble machine and made some beautiful plastic bubbles. He blew into the pipe and sent the elevator shooting up.

At the PPP table, he fiddled with the radio controls and sent the paper airplane flying back and forth across the science lab. Then he picked up the clump of dust from my hand and squeezed it a few times. "Clever," he muttered. "Totally clever."

Finally he tested the two-sided toothbrush. He

pushed it into his mouth and moved it up and down. After a few seconds, he started to scream:

"HELP!
STUCK!
STUCK!
HELLLP!
MMMMMPH!
MMMMPH!"

It took everyone awhile to realize the toothbrush was stuck in his mouth. Finally two kids rushed forward and pulled with all their might.

POPPPPPPPP!

The brush flew out with a spray of blood. Mr. Spittup's gums were bleeding and his lip was cut.

Mr. Spittup mopped his mouth with a wad of tissues. "I think I know which school will be heading home," he said. "You kids with the stupid toothbrush from Whussup School. Whussup with you? You're outta here! Go pack your bags!"

We kids from the other four schools all cheered and jumped up and down and slapped high fives and touched knuckles. I watched the Whussup kids slump out of the room with their heads down.

I shook my head. "They just didn't have a good idea," I told my buddies. "Not like us."

I held up the dust clump—but a gust of wind from an open window blew it away. "Belzer," I said, "collect more dust. We've got a winner here!"

"Who invented dust?" Belzer asked. "That's a good invention! You see it everywhere!"

I patted Belzer on the head. "Take it easy, Belzer," I said. "Just get a nice big hunk of dust for the finals tomorrow."

I hurried to the door.

"Bernie, where are you going?" Crench called. "Don't you want to celebrate our victory?"

"No time," I said. "Feldspar Pyrite invited me to a croquet game. I think he might want to make a little friendly bet on it. That's how I'm gonna celebrate. I'm gonna take his money!"

"But, Bernie—" Crench called. "Have you ever played croquet in your life?"

"How hard could it be?" I said. "You hit something with something—right? Easy!"

Little did I realize I was about to be punk'd and skunked in a big way!

Chapter 19

A CROQUET LESSON

I found the Croquet Lawn just past the Rose Garden. The ground was flat, and the grass was cut short. The silver wickets gleamed in the bright sunshine.

No one was here yet. I picked up a wooden mallet and did a few practice swings. "Go easy on them, Bernie," I told myself. "I'll give them a little lesson in how the game is played. But I won't be mean and run up a big score."

I leaned forward and swung the mallet hard.

"OWWWWW!"

I accidentally smacked it into my ankle. Pain shot up my leg.

I was still hopping on one foot when Feldspar, Alli, and Corky appeared.

"Bernie, are you okay?" Alli asked.

I hopped a few more times, rubbing my ankle. "Just doing my warm-up exercises," I said. "Gotta be loose for this game—right?"

Alli checked her clipboard. "I have ten minutes and forty-two seconds to play," she said. "So let's get started." She picked up a mallet and stepped up to the first pole.

Feldspar flashed me an evil smile. "Bernie, what do you say? How about a dollar a wicket?"

I liked this kid. He was tricky. But I *like* tricky.

I grinned back at him. "I hate taking your money," I said. "But maybe I can give you a few pointers in this game."

His grin grew wider. "You don't stand a chance," he said. "I've been playing croquet since I was a baby. Before I learned to walk, I had to butt the ball with my little baby head."

Was he *serious*?

"Pigges have been playing this game for two hundred years," Corky said. "We helped to invent the mallet. Before mallets, no one could figure out how to hit the ball."

These kids were *tough* when it came to croquet. But I knew I had something on my side—the Bernie Bridges luck. I couldn't lose!

We all shook hands. The bet was on.

Alli was about to swing her mallet. But Corky grabbed her arm. "Let Bernie go first," he said. "He's our guest."

Corky set down a bright blue ball for me. Then he backed away quickly.

Everyone backed away. They were giving me plenty of room. I guessed they wanted a good view of a master player. They were staring hard.

I didn't want to disappoint them. I tapped the ball a few times. Then I gave it a hard wallop and—

BAARRROOOOM!

Chapter 20

A RULE AGAINST NAKED BUTTS?

The blast sent me staggering backward. I felt my *hair* fly up on my head. My arms flew up, and I started flapping them like a bird.

I staggered in circles. The sound of the explosion rang in my ears. And when I finally stopped teetering and tottering and looked down, *my clothes were gone!*

I stood there on the grass in my underpants!

Dizzy, I spun around—and saw the three Prepsters laughing their heads off. They were slapping high fives and touching knuckles. And pointing at the

tatters of my clothes on the grass.

"Ha-ha. Funny," I choked out. My voice cracked. My knees wobbled. My ears still rang.

"We didn't tell you about Corky's hobby," Feldspar said. "He likes to blow things up."

"Nothing personal," Alli said. "He does it to everyone."

"Th-that's the LAST thing I'd expect Corky to d-do," I stammered.

Corky smiled and stuck his little nose in the air. "Pigges have been blowing things up for two hundred years," he said proudly. "We helped invent dynamite. Before that, people had to shout *BANG* at each other!"

"Well, thanks for the game," I said. "You guys are real good sports."

Punk'd and skunked AGAIN!

On the tennis court, kids stopped to stare at me in my underpants. And I heard kids laughing from the Rose Garden.

I turned and started to jog to the dorm—and ran right into Headmaster Snute.

His eyes bulged, his mouth shot open, and he

made a gurgling sound. He dropped his fishing rod and pointed at me. "Aren't you one of those Rotten School kids?" he asked. "Why are you dressed like that?"

Think fast, Bernie. Think fast.

"Uh...well...I'm just working on a *new* invention, sir," I said. "Testing the elastic on these underpants. Uh...if the elastic holds, I think you'll be amazed at what we can do."

He stared at me for a long time. "I hope the elastic holds, too," he said finally. "We don't allow naked butts at Preppy Prep Prep. Read the rule book. It's on page one."

He picked up his fishing rod. "There's a fish tank in the library," he said. "I'm going fishing for angelfish. Ever try to catch one? They put up a good fight."

"Good luck, sir," I said. I turned and ran to the dorm. I ignored all the hoots and shouts and laughs from the kids I passed.

Luckily, the elastic on my underpants held...

...almost until I reached the dorm.

Chapter 21

SWEET!

Kids sat in a wide circle on the lawn to watch the Make-a-Great-Invention Contest. White, puffy clouds floated across the sky. Robins twittered in the trees. Butterflies fluttered over the Rose Garden.

I have to admit I had butterflies, too. In my stomach. Yes, I know. Bernie B. never gets stressed. But let me tell you, I was a little nervous today.

I had a big clump of dust in my backpack. Next to me were the Poly-Wannacracker dudes with the plastic bubble-blowing machine. Then the PPP guys with the radio-controlled paper airplane. Down at the end stood the Baked Potato Chips kids with their amazing human-breath elevator.

How could I win with a hunk of dust? Even Bernie the Great was stressed to the max.

Alli Katz and Corky Pigge came by. They both wished me good luck. Corky winked at me for some reason, and flashed me a thumbs-up. What was *that* about?

Mr. Snute stepped up to the microphone. "Before I introduce the judges," he said, "I want to show you all something." He held up a wooden plaque. I could see a small fish shellacked onto the front of the plaque.

"Here is the goldfish I caught last week," he announced. "Biggest goldfish I ever nabbed—almost two inches long! This one is going up in my living room!"

He set the plaque down carefully. Then he turned back to the microphone. "We have four wonderful inventions competing for the five-thousand-dollar prize," he announced.

I pulled the dust clump from my backpack and smoothed it out. Would it work this time? Did I have a winner here?

"I'd like to introduce the judges," Mr. Snute said. "First of all—"

Those were the only words he got out.

BARRRROOOOOOOOM!

A deafening roar dropped me to the ground. The earth shook. A thick cloud of white smoke covered everyone.

Coughing and choking, still on my hands and knees, I opened my eyes and gazed at the sky. It was RAINING INVENTIONS!

The elevator had broken into a hundred pieces. I saw the paper airplane wings fly off in different directions. Plastic bubbles floated down. The bubble maker came crashing down next to me with a deafening *CRUNCH!*

Kids ducked and covered their heads.

Whoa. My brain began to spin. The other three inventions had been *blown to bits.*

I glanced at my fist and saw that my dust clump hadn't been harmed.

Yes! YES!! Brilliant move, Bernie! Good news! You *can't* blow up DUST!!

Corky Pigge stood at the back of the crowd, laughing his Pigge head off. He gave me the thumbs-up sign. That dude really does like to blow up things. Weird.

Mr. Snute was talking with the judges, waving his arms, shaking his head. After a few minutes he stepped back to the microphone.

"Settle down, people," he shouted. "I don't want anyone to worry. My fish plaque is perfectly okay. Not a scratch."

He held up the goldfish plaque so we could all see that it was not harmed. Then he continued: "I'm sorry to say, after that unexpected explosion, we have only one invention left. The Instant Dust from Rotten School. It's a horrible, stupid invention. But we have no choice. Rotten School wins the prize!"

My buddies and I were the only ones who cheered. What a bunch of sore losers!

But we didn't care. We hooted and hollered, slapped knuckles, and did the secret Rotten House handshake. Then we went outside and took a few victory laps around the track.

Victory is sweet. SWEET!

Chapter 22

A Big Finish

The four of us returned to Rotten School as winners. WINNERS! What a beautiful word! Almost as beautiful as one other word—BERNIE.

Headmaster Upchuck met us at the front gate as our bus pulled up. He gave us a warm greeting: "I'm really sorry to see you boys back," he said.

I waved the winning check in front of me. "We won, sir!" I cried. "We won five thousand dollars."

He snatched the check out of my hand. "Thank you, Bernie. I'm going to put this to good use."

"Huh?" I gasped. "Y-you mean … we don't get to *keep* it?"

"Of course not," Upchuck said. "The money goes to improve the school." He tucked the check into his jacket pocket. "I think I know a *good* improvement for the school. A flat-screen TV for my den."

"But—but—but—" I sputtered.

Headmaster Upchuck studied us. "I hope your stay at Preppy Prep Prep improved you boys," he said.

"Oh, yes, sir," I replied. "It taught us a lot. We're going to be very different now. In fact, I'm starting a croquet team. I hope you'll come watch us play."

Upchuck smiled. "Yes. Croquet. That's more like it, Bernie."

I pulled a bright blue croquet ball from my backpack. "Check it out, sir. A special ball we brought back."

"Hand me that mallet," the Headmaster said. "Let me try it out. Croquet was my sport in college."

"No, wait, sir—" I said. "Please—no—"

Too late.

Upchuck set the ball down. He swung the mallet.

He slammed the ball. And guess what? It DIDN'T explode!

For nearly two seconds.

Then...

BAAAAARRRRRR~
OOOOOOM!

I like a story with a surprise ending—don't you?

HERE'S A SNEAK PEEK AT BOOK #12

R.L. STINE'S

GOOD
MEMORIES

I ran up the two flights of stairs to my room. Feenman and Crench's room is across the hall from mine. I could hear loud shouts and screams inside.

Probably doing their Three Stooges act, I decided. Feenman and Crench love to kick and slap and head-butt each other and poke each other's eyes out. It's a total riot—especially if you like pain.

I pushed open the door and stepped inside their room. A blast of hot, steamy air hit my face. It's always hot in there. Their room used to be a closet.

"Whoa! I don't believe this!" I cried.

Feenman and Crench weren't poking and slapping each other. They were hunched over a laptop, staring at the screen. Crench frantically moved the mouse, clicking it again and again.

The shouts and cries came from the laptop.

"Give me a break," I said, stepping up beside them. "What's up with this?"

Feenman raised a finger to his lips. "*Shhhh*. It's the Battle of Heartburnia."

I gasped. "The WHAT??"

He shushed me again.

An armored knight on the screen had a long spear shoved through his chest. It went all the way through him and came out the other side.

"YOOOOWWWWWW!" Feenman screamed, as if he was the one who got skewered.

"Bet that hurts," I muttered.

Feenman held his chest, gasping for air.

"Want a Band-aid?" I asked.

"*Shhhh*." It was Crench's turn to shush me. He had his face right up against the screen. He clicked the mouse furiously. "Gotcha! Gotcha! Gotcha!" he screamed.

"We have to use our swords," Feenman told me. "We don't have enough weapon points to buy fireballs."

"We spent all our bubus on a horse," Crench said.

CLICK CLICK CLICK CLICK.

"You WHAT?" I cried. "Spent all your bubus? Have you both gone nuts?"

CLICK CLICK CLICK CLICK.

"Will you two stop?" I screamed.

They both spun around. Crench kept clicking the mouse. I guess he couldn't stop his finger.

"We can't take a break in the middle of a battle," Crench said. "Do you want our knights to lose the big wing-wang?"

"Stop talking baby talk!" I shouted. "You're starting to scare me. I need you guys for a real-life emergency."

Feenman scratched his head. "Real life?"

"We can't help you," Crench said. "We're the Doo-Wah-Diddy Dragons."

Feenman nodded. His hair fell over his face. He looked a lot better that way.

"The Doo-Wah-Diddy Dragons are battling the Knighty Knight Knights," he said.

4

I pinched their cheeks. "You two are definitely dum diddys," I said. "How can you waste your time on a stupid game?"

"It isn't a game," Crench said. "It's a battle to the death. If the Knighty Knight Knights win the Battle of Heartburnia, we'll have to pay a battle tax to the Great Wungo Wango."

I slapped my forehead. "Please—speak English! What's wrong with you two?"

CLICK CLICK CLICK CLICK.

"Listen to me, dudes," I said. "Remember what I overheard in Upchuck's office? The inspectors are coming on Saturday, and they're going to shut down the school. We've got to act fast. Don't you want to go to your next school with your pockets full of bubus?"

CLICK CLICK CLICK.

Okay. That didn't work. I decided to try a different approach.

"Don't you care about your school?" I asked. "Don't you have any feelings at all for this wonderful place? Don't you have any heart?"

They both turned away from the laptop and stared at me.

I put my arms around their shoulders. "We're good buddies, right?" I said. "And we've had wonderful times here. Great, great memories." I let a few tears fall from my eyes.

"You okay, Bernie?" Feenman asked.

"I...I just can't believe our school could be gone in a few days," I said. I let my voice tremble. "Don't you guys remember all the good times? Remember when Headmaster Upchuck fell in Pooper's Pond and we had to pull a minnow out of his nose? Remember when Mrs. Heinie lost her glasses and walked right into a bulldozer? Remember when the chef accidentally put poison ivy in the salad?"

"Good times," Crench said.

"Yeah. Lotsa good memories," Feenman said.

"Well, don't you want to cash in before the good memories are gone forever?" I asked.

CLICK CLICK CLICK CLICK CLICK.

ABOUT THE AUTHOR

R.L. Stine graduated from Rotten School with a solid D+ average, which put him at the top of his class. He says that his favorite activities at school were Scratching Body Parts and Making Armpit Noises.

In sixth grade, R.L. won the school Athletic Award for his performance in the Wedgie Championships. Unfortunately, after the tournament, his underpants had to be surgically removed.

After graduation, R.L. became well known for writing scary book series such as The Nightmare Room, Fear Street, Goosebumps, and Mostly Ghostly, and a short story collection called Beware!

Today, R.L. lives in New York City, where he is busy writing stories about his school days.

For more information about R.L. Stine,
go to www.rottenschool.com
and www.rlstine.com